Merry Hiss-Mas

Written and illustrated by Steve Hyde

To ....

From ....

For Ananya

ISBN: 9798357741066

One night in December, it started to snow

Sammy the Snake was enjoying the show

Ssso pretty, he hissed, I can't wait to go out

Do some sssking and sssledging and ssslithering about

"Silly snake!" said his owner, "you can't go out there!"

"A cold-blooded snake won't survive the cold air!

You just stay by the fire where it's toasty and nice

Keep away from that horrible cold snow and ice!"

Sammy was sad, but knew Sarah was right

He wasn't equipped for a cold winter's night

If a human needs such a big thick snuggly jacket

There's no way a cold-blooded reptile could hack it

But Sammy thought Yesss! I know what I can do!

I'll wrap myself up in warm winter clothes too!

But he couldn't really move in a thick Christmas
sweater

And a warm pair of mittens didn't work any better

Wearing a scarf as a snake can be tough...

...and earmuffs don't work with no ears to muff

I give up, thought the snake, there's nothing I can wear

That will fit well enough to keep me warm out there.

So he laid by the fire for a pre-Christmas nap...

...until he was awoken by a sharp TAP TAP TAP!

"Go to sleep!" smiled Sarah, "it's only me!

I'm hanging out stockings for Santa, you see"

But Sammy was suddenly fully awake

That's no ssstocking....

...it's a sssnuggly sssweater for a sssnake!

He slid into the stocking then out of the door

Feeling warm and excited like never before

He built his first snowman that very same night...

...made his first snake-snow-angel...

...had his first snowball fight.

He was cosy and comfy and no longer sad...

'Twas the MERRIEST HISS-MAS a snake ever had!

Merry Hiss-Mas!

Please consider leaving a review on Amazon if you enjoyed this book. Reviews help readers find this book and anything else I publish in future

See how this book came together using the QR code link above

Twitter: @stevenjameshyde

Printed in Great Britain
by Amazon